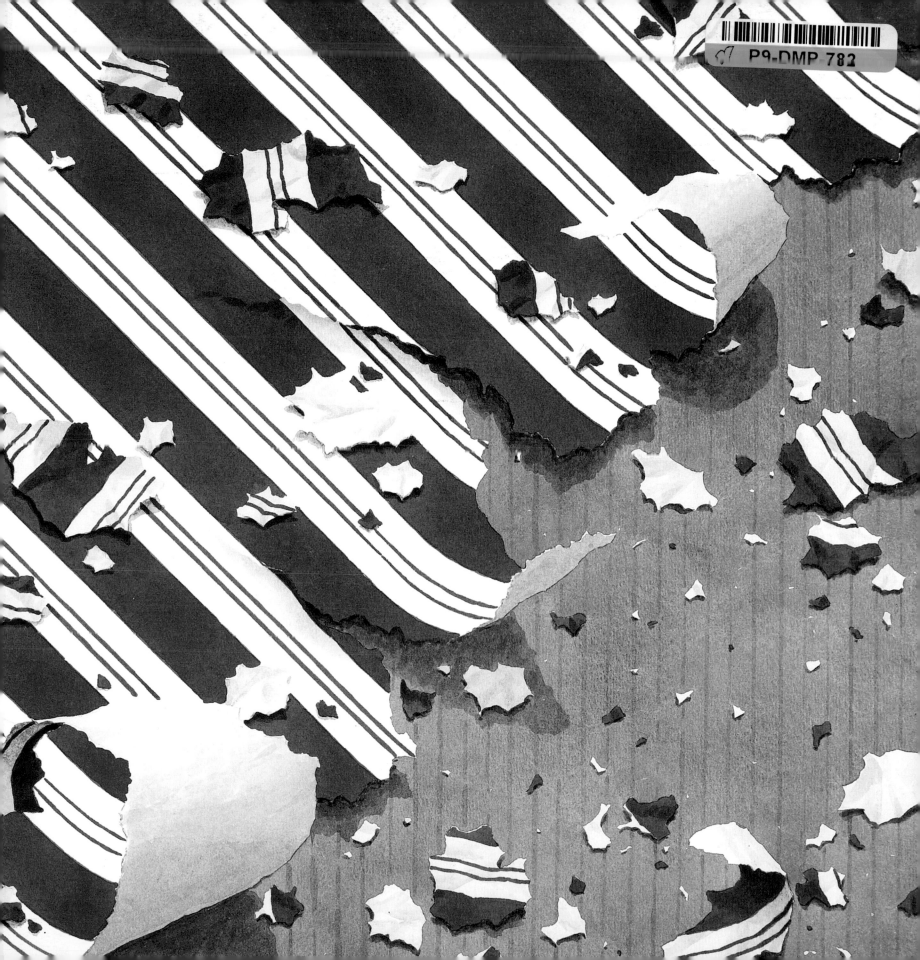

For all the world's Marleys, and the families that love them.
—J.G.

To Lauren, Megan, Allie, and Ryan,
for all the wonderful Christmas memories.
Love, Dad
—R.C.

A Very Marley Christmas
Text and art copyright © 2008 by John Grogan

Printed in the U.S.A.
All rights reserved. No part of this book may be used or reproduced in any
manner whatsoever without written permission except in the case of brief
quotations embodied in critical articles and reviews. For information address
HarperCollins Children's Books, a division of HarperCollins Publishers,
1350 Avenue of the Americas, New York, NY 10019.
www.harpercollinschildrens.com

Library of Congress Cataloging-in-Publication Data is available.
ISBN 978-0-06-137292-6 (trade bdg.) — ISBN 978-0-06-137293-3 (lib. bdg.)

Typography by Jeanne L. Hogle
1 2 3 4 5 6 7 8 9 10
❖
First Edition

John Grogan

A Very Marley Christmas

illustrated by Richard Cowdrey

HarperCollinsPublishers

hristmas was fast approaching at the little house on Churchill Road. Cassie and Baby Louie wanted everything to be just right for Santa's big visit, but something was missing: snow.

"C'mon, snow! Let's go!" Cassie said.

"Ya ya, zo! Eek oh!" Baby Louie said.

Their big yellow puppy, Marley, pushed his giant head between theirs and stared out the window, whimpering softly.

"Arrrooof!" he said.

But no flakes came.

"The snow will come when the snow is ready," Daddy said.

"Come on, kids," said Mommy. "Let's get the house ready for Santa."

This was Marley's very first Christmas, and he wanted everything to be ready too. He jumped in to help in every way he could. But Marley, being Marley, always ended up on the wrong side of right.

That afternoon Daddy brought home a big evergreen tree. But as he dragged it across the lawn to the house, the tree suddenly stopped.

It would not drag.

It would not slide.

It would not budge.

Daddy pulled; the tree pulled back. Daddy yanked harder; the tree yanked back harder.

"What the heck?" Daddy said.

Then he saw the problem.

Marley never could pass up a good game of tug-of-war.

"Bad dog, Marley!" Daddy yelled.

"Let go!"

Mommy strung colored lights on the bushes outside. Finally, she got them just the way she wanted. "Perfect!" she said.

But Marley had other ideas.
"Bad dog, Marley!" Mommy yelled.

Cassie was inside cutting out a chain of paper snowflakes to hang in the window. She was nearly done when Marley came around the corner and spotted the giant slithering white serpent.

I'll save you! Marley seemed to say.

With three big leaps across the room, he attacked Cassie's masterpiece. "Woof! Grrrrrrr! Snap!" And that was the end of the paper snowflakes.

"You big goof, Marley!" Cassie yelled. "Can't you tell a snow*flake* from a snow *snake*?"

Baby Louie painted a picture of a snowman for the front door.
Hooray! thought Marley. *I love to make art!*

"Baa boo-boo, Waddy!" Louie yelled.

Daddy called from the living room, "Tree's up!"
Everyone came running. Marley came running too.
Mommy stopped.
Cassie stopped.
Baby Louie stopped.
Marley did not stop.

Oops! No brakes!

Daddy got the tree back up. *Sniff, sniff, sniff*. For Marley, Christmas had come early. *Finally! My very own indoor bathroom!*

"Waddy wee-wee!" Baby Louie screeched.

Cassie decorated the tree with ornaments, but the ornaments did not stay on the tree for long.

"Drop it, Marley!" Cassie said.

Daddy opened the tinsel. Marley dove right in to decorate.

Mommy hung a stocking above the fireplace for each member of the family. Marley thought it would be more fun to play elephant. He wiggled his snout deep inside the sock and charged blindly through the house.

"Marley stampede!" Cassie yelled. "Take cover!"

At last everything was just right. Everything except for one thing. The most important decoration of all was still missing. It was Christmas Eve, and the fluffy white stuff had not arrived.

"How can Santa land his sleigh without snow?" Cassie asked.

"Zoey! Zo! Zo!" Louie scolded the sky.

Daddy kissed Cassie on the forehead. "Have you been good?" he asked.

"I've tried," Cassie said. "Really, really tried."

"Then Santa won't forget you, snow or no snow."

"And he won't forget my toboggan?" she asked.

"Let's keep our fingers crossed," Daddy said.

"Okay, kiddos, time for bed," Mommy said. "Santa won't come until everyone is asleep."

Cassie and Louie peered out the window one last time.

"No zo," Baby Louie said with a sigh.

The next morning, Cassie and Louie were the first ones awake. They jumped on Mommy and Daddy's bed and begged to go downstairs. Marley was up too, stretching and banging his tail against the mattress like it was a kettledrum. *Thump! Thump! Thump!*

"Please, please, please!" Cassie said.

"Peas! Peas! Peas!" Louie said.

"Ruff! Ruff! Ruff!" Marley said.

Daddy tried to roll over and close his eyes, but falling back asleep was *not* an option.

"Let's go see if Santa came," Mommy said.

Marley led the way.

The living room was filled with toys and presents of
every shape and size.

"He was here!" Cassie exclaimed. "Santa came!"

"What did I tell you?" Daddy said.

Just then, from the window near the tree, came
a giant commotion. Half of Marley was
sticking out of the closed curtains. Both
halves were making a terrible fuss.

"Get out of there, you nutty dog!"
Mommy ordered.

"What is it, Big Guy?" Cassie
asked.

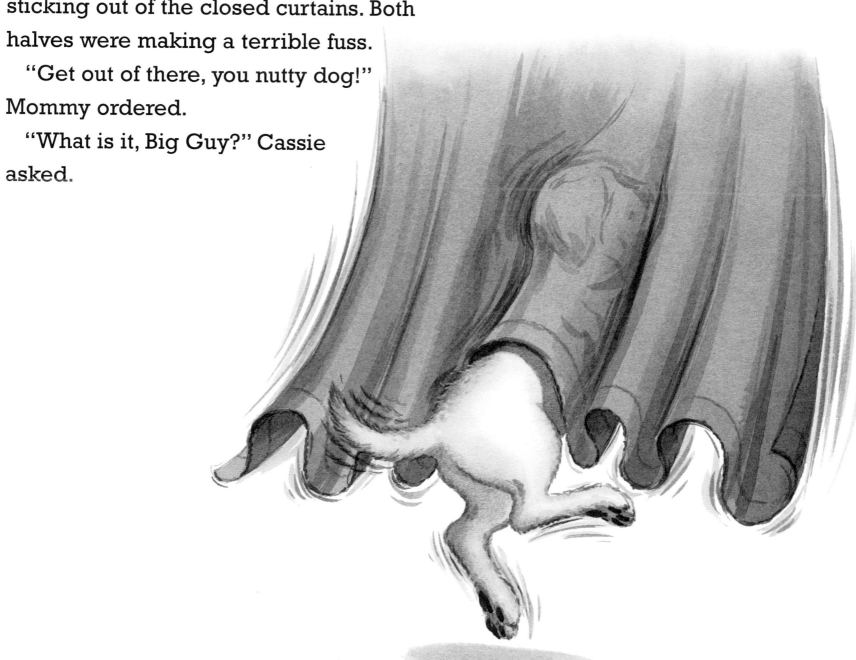

She pulled back the curtains, and there it was. Falling from the sky. Blanketing the ground. Powdering the pine trees. Drifting over the driveway, hiding the hedges, and burying the bushes.

Snow.

Marley jumped on his hind legs and yelped proudly
as if he had delivered it himself. *Your wish is my
command!* he seemed to say.

Cassie threw open the front door.

"Yessss!" she shouted. "Yippee!"

"Zubby zoey zo zo!" Baby Louie screeched.

Just then a yellow blur streaked past.

It knocked Baby Louie smack down on his giant, droopy diaper and shot straight out the door. Marley had never felt snow before. *Ah! Wet! Ah! Cold!* He slammed on the brakes. This was not a good idea.

Marley went into a full skid, flopped onto one side, bounced up again, spun twice, then somersaulted down the front steps and into a deep snowdrift.

The whole family held its breath.

When he finally popped his head up, Marley looked like a giant powdered doughnut.

Marley raced past Cassie. He raced past Baby Louie. He raced past Mommy and Daddy and straight into the living room. He jumped on the new toboggan and shook the biggest shake of his life. Snow flew everywhere!

Even Mommy had to laugh.

Santa had brought the best gift of all—and his helper Marley had delivered it inside.

"Zoey zoey zo zo!" Baby Louie shouted. "Good bow-wow, Waddy!"

"Have a Very Marley Christmas!"